Zorgan and the Gorsemen

www.charmseekers.co.uk

CHARMSEEKERS: BOOK TWELVE

Zorgan and the Gorsemen

Georgie Adams

Illustrated by Gwen Millward

Orion
Children's Books

First published in Great Britain in 2009
by Orion Children's Books
Reissued 2012 by Orion Children's Books
a division of the Orion Publishing Group Ltd
Orion House
5 Upper St Martin's Lane
London WC2H 9EA
An Hachette UK Company

1 3 5 7 9 8 6 4 2

The Orion Publishing Group's policy is to use papers
that are natural, renewable and recyclable products
and made from wood grown in sustainable forests. The logging
and manufacturing processes are expected to conform to
the environmental regulations of the country of origin.

A catalogue record for this book is
available from the British Library.

ISBN 978 1 4440 0300 0

Printed and bound in by
CPI Group (UK) Ltd, Croydon, CR0 4YY

www.orionbooks.co.uk
www.charmseekers.co.uk

For Jonathan and Jenny with love

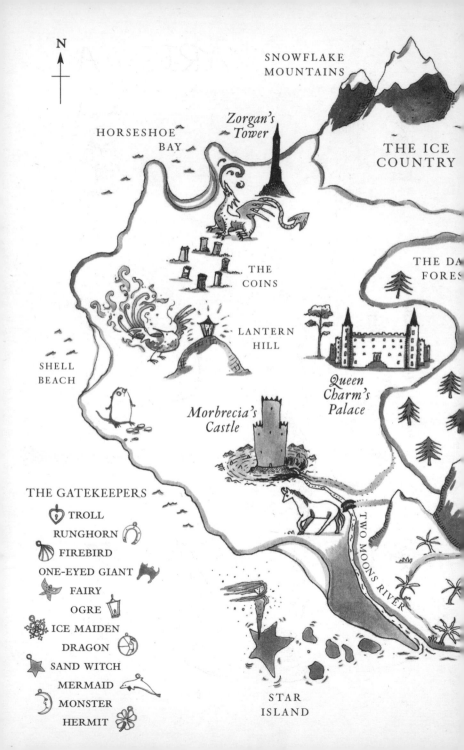

KARISMA

CAPE CAT

CLOVER FIELDS

HEARTMOOR

DOLPHIN BAY

MOUNT FORTUNA

The Silver Pool

KEY POINT

SWAMPS

MERMAID ROCK

JUNGLE

BUTTERFLY BAY

The Thirteen Charms of Karisma

When Charm became queen of Karisma, the wise and beautiful Silversmith made her a precious gift. It was a bracelet. On it were fastened thirteen silver amulets, which the Silversmith called 'charms', in honour of the new queen.

It was part of Karisma law. Whenever there was a new ruler the Silversmith made a special gift, to help them care for the world they had inherited. And this time it was a bracelet. She told Queen Charm it was magical because the charms held the power to control the forces of nature and keep everything in balance. She must take the greatest care of them. As long as she, and she alone, had possession of the charms all would be well.

And so it was, until the bracelet was stolen by a spider, and fell into the hands of Zorgan, the magician. Then there was chaos!

One

Sesame was trapped in Zorgan's Tower! The witch had slammed the door shut and turned the key. From a window, Sesame saw her sitting astride a broomstick, her tattered black rags flapping like the wings of a crow.

Sesame couldn't believe she'd been tricked so easily into parting with the magical charm bracelet. By chance, she'd met a beautiful young woman with long, silvery hair and sparkling eyes walking near Queen Charm's palace. The friendly stranger had called herself the Silversmith and promised to return the bracelet to the queen.

Sesame believed her, but as soon as she had taken hold of the bracelet, the woman changed into an ugly witch! Next thing she knew, Sesame was locked in the magician's tower, with no idea how she'd got there. She was very, very frightened.

Suddenly the witch flew to the window and Sesame stared in horror at her ghastly face, which was more wrinkled than an old potato. The hag gloated at Sesame through the glass. From a bony finger, she dangled the silver charm bracelet . . .

"Give it back!" cried Sesame. "Let me go!"

The witch cackled.

"Foolish child," she croaked. "I'll do no such thing. I've no further use for you. Soon you'll be nothing but a heap of bones, Sesame Brown! *Sesame—*"

"—Sesame, come *down*! Breakfast's ready!"

Sesame woke to hear her dad, Nic Brown, calling from downstairs. She sat up, shook her head and realised everything had been a ghastly nightmare. Her digital alarm clock was buzzing on her bedside table. It was 9:10 A.M. She pressed the stop button and jumped out of bed.

"Coming, Dad! Be down in five!"

The nightmare had been *so* real! Sesame knew she was being silly, but she opened her special jewellery box, to check the charm bracelet was still inside.

4

It was. Eleven, glistening silver charms were fastened to the silver band, safe and sound. Happily she closed the lid and went to the window. It was a sunny Saturday morning and there wasn't a witch in the sky – just a fluffy white cloud, which Sesame thought looked like four-leafed clover. A lucky sign. And she would be riding her favourite pony, Silver, at Jodie Luck's stables in less than an hour.

"I can't wait to ride!" she told her teddy, Alfie.

Dashing to the bathroom to wash, Sesame told herself to stop thinking about Zorgan and his stories about the Silversmith. But ever since her last adventure in Karisma,* she couldn't help wondering if the Silversmith really *was* a wicked witch. No wonder I'm having weird dreams, she thought. She washed and brushed her teeth, then paused to look in the mirror.

* *
*Do you remember what happened? You can follow Sesame's last adventure in Karisma in Book Eleven: *The Mirror of Deception*

"Nothing is going to stop me looking for the charms," she said. "I've only two more to find. Sesame Brown will track them down!"

A few minutes later, she was pulling on her jodhpurs, shirt and riding boots in record time. Then, remembering to put on her favourite necklace with a locket, she raced down to the kitchen.

✳ ✳ ✳

After breakfast, Nic drove Sesame to the stables. On the way they talked about the barbeque Nic had planned for that afternoon.

"I've texted Maddy, Gemma and Liz," said Sesame. "They can come."

"Great," said Nic. "I've invited some friends. They're looking forward to meeting Jodie. I can't believe we've been going out for nearly a year!"

"Brill," agreed Sesame. She was very fond of her riding teacher; for some time she'd been wondering how she would feel if her dad and Jodie decided to marry. Sitting in the back of the car, Sesame started to daydream. Her mum, Poppy, had died when she was a baby, but she still felt loyal to her. It would feel strange to have a new mum around. Nevertheless, she found herself hoping Poppy wouldn't have minded about Jodie, because she *was* really nice . . .

Soon Nic turned off the busy road and drove down a rough track, flanked by neatly-fenced paddocks, to the stables. While he was parking the car, Sesame saw Olivia Pike – a girl she knew from school, who kept her own pony, Misty Morning, at Jodie's livery stables. Olivia was very snobbish and Sesame didn't like her at all. Her mother, Mrs Pike, was talking to Jodie and,

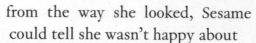

from the way she looked, Sesame could tell she wasn't happy about something. After a brief conversation Jodie hurried over to them, her soft blue eyes flashing with fury.

"Problems?" said Nic. He thought Jodie looked even more attractive when she was angry.

"Mrs Pike insists there's been a mix-up over Olivia's riding lesson," said Jodie. "She *says* she booked a lesson for ten o'clock. I checked. It was for eleven. But if I don't agree to change it, she's threatened to take Misty away and keep him at another stable—"

"The old witch," mumbled Sesame.

"Ses!" warned Nic. "Don't be rude."

"I've sorted it," said Jodie, "but I'm afraid you'll have to wait for your ride this morning, Sesame."

"That's okay," said Sesame. She was disappointed, but she knew it wasn't Jodie's fault. "I'll help around the stables while I'm waiting."

"Good," said Nic. "See you later. Don't be late for the barbeque. I'm cooking!"

Jodie gave him a quick kiss.

"I'll bring Sesame home," she said. "Don't worry. We'll be there in good time!"

Two

While Olivia was enjoying her riding lesson, Sesame busied herself grooming ponies. She had just finished brushing Silver, when she saw Olivia leading Misty Morning into his stable. Mrs Pike was close behind, click-clacking across the cobbled yard in high-heels, chivvying her daughter along. She had a shrill voice and Sesame overheard her say:

"Hurry up, Olivia. I mustn't be late for my hair appointment. Raymondo is doing my highlights today."

"Yes, Mummy," said Olivia. "But I must give Misty some water—"

Mrs Pike looked at her watch.

"We haven't got time!" she said impatiently.

Sesame frowned.

"Mrs Pike is more concerned about her hair than caring for Misty!" she whispered to Silver, as she shut his stable door. It occurred to her that maybe Mrs Pike had wangled an earlier lesson for Olivia, so *she* could get to the hairdressers. A few minutes later, she watched them roar off in a four-by-four, leaving clouds of dust. Jodie came over to Sesame, sighing with relief.

"Now you can have your ride," she said. "Shall we tack Silver up?"

"Er . . . I should water Misty first," said Sesame.

"Why?" asked Jodie. "Surely Olivia saw to him before she left?"

Sesame hadn't *meant* to get Olivia into trouble. Reluctantly she told Jodie what had happened.

"You wait till I see Mrs—"
Jodie began, and then
stopped.

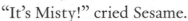

They heard a clatter of
hooves on the cobbles
and saw a pony bolting
across the yard.

"It's Misty!" cried Sesame.

"He's making for the road!" shouted Jodie.

Sesame pelted after the runaway pony, taking
a shortcut across a paddock. She reached the
end of the drive in time to see Misty Morning
disappearing behind a hedge near the road.

"Misty! Come back," she yelled.

Next instant, she heard the blare of a car horn, the
squeal of tyres, someone shouting. Sesame skidded
round a corner, her heart thudding. The traffic had
come to a halt and, to her immense relief, she saw
Olivia's pony standing by the hedge – his dappled-
grey coat damp with sweat, eyes wide with fright.

Keep calm, Sesame told herself, as slowly she approached him. "It's okay, Misty," she said softly. "Stay. *Please* stay . . ." Suddenly Misty threw up his head and looked as if he was about to bolt again, when Sesame grabbed him by the mane. Which was when Jodie came running up with a halter.

"Well done, Ses!" she said, as they walked him back to the yard. "I couldn't have managed without you."

It took a while for them to settle the pony in his stable, so there wasn't time for Sesame to ride. Jodie promised to arrange another lesson very soon, then she rang Mrs Pike on her mobile.

"*So* sorry to interrupt your hair appointment," she said. "But there's something we should talk about . . . NOW!"

✻ ✻ ✻

They arrived at Sesame's house after everyone else, and found the garden full of people. Jodie caught sight of Nic squirting water on the barbeque flames. He waved to them through a haze of smoke and Jodie hurried off to help him.

Sesame spotted her friends by the apple tree, and raced across the lawn to greet them.

"Hi, Ses," cried Gemma.

"We thought you weren't coming," said Liz.

"We've been here *ages*," complained Maddy. "Only joking – *I'm* the one who's usually late!"

Sesame gave her best friend a hug.

"Sorry," she said. "Jodie and I had stuff to do at the stables."

Then she noticed her friends were wearing funky shorts, skirts and tops.

"I'll just change out of my riding gear," she said. "I won't be long—"

She was turning to go, when she was distracted by a prickling sensation at the nape of her neck. She held her locket and felt its familiar tingle, the way it did when something extraordinary was about to happen. Butterflies tickled her tummy. Goose pimples prickled her arms. Sesame saw pink, green and blue wisps of smoke, coiling and curling into a misty rainbow, swirling faster and faster, until her head was spinning and she felt her feet leave the ground. The others were caught up in it too and she heard their voices, floating to her from a distance:

"What's happening?"

"I'm flying!"

"I feel *weird*!"

The last thing she remembered was Maddy grabbing her hand, before they all floated up through the branches of the apple tree. Soon they were flying over the rooftops, whisked through the air on a magical rainbow, to the amazing world of Karisma.

14

Three

Zorgan had been in a foul temper ever since he'd failed to fool Sesame with his twisted stories about the Silversmith. She had stubbornly refused to believe him and secretly, he admitted to himself she had courage, but he had no intention of giving up.

"I'll find a way to break her will," he stormed over and over again. "Just wait till she returns!"

While the magician was waiting, he amused himself by inflicting spells on the innocent, unsuspecting people of Karisma: snowstorms on a summer's day, for example, and frightening nightmares.

It cheered him to see their discomfort. He was particularly pleased with a plague of mice he'd conjured, which had invaded the palace. Zorgan enjoyed observing them through his crystal ball;

the rodents were running amok in the royal household, causing no end of trouble. But the day before Sesame and her friends arrived in Karisma, he learned some disturbing news . . .

Queen Charm had called a Kluster,* to discuss the worsening state of affairs. Among her officials were the Chancellor, a stout man called Robustus, and Officer Dork; also there was Zorgan's old enemy, the Silversmith. Through the power of his magical sphere, Zorgan overheard every word . . .

"Zorgan is causing mayhem with his magic, Your Majesty. The palace is alive with mice! I found one in my soup today. Ugh!"

"Yes, the magician is making our lives a misery. I've been having terrible nightmares. Scary they were. It's time for action!"

"Sesame had a lucky escape last time she was here. I dread to think what Zorgan will try next. He's determined to get hold of the charms . . ."

* *
* **Kluster** – a meeting of important officials

17

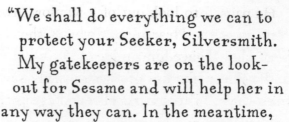

"We shall do everything we can to protect your Seeker, Silversmith. My gatekeepers are on the look-out for Sesame and will help her in any way they can. In the meantime, the magician remains a threat. I had hoped we could resolve things peacefully. But enough is enough! Zorgan MUST be punished. Officer Dork, take him by force without delay!"

Zorgan couldn't believe his ears.

"Foolish queen!" he screamed at his crystal ball, as if Charm could hear him. "You dare to challenge ME? Dork doesn't stand a chance against my magical powers."

Nevertheless, Charm's words had given him cause for concern. Zorgan paced the floor of his Star Room, considering what to do.

"Forewarned is forearmed," he muttered. "I mustn't risk anything ruining my plans. When I have the fabulous bracelet, I'll empower it with Dark Magic. Morbrecia will become queen and wear it, but *I* shall control the charms and rule Karisma!"

18

He paused to look out of a window. Away in the distance was Heartmoor, where the Gorsemen lived, and it gave him an idea.

"I could make use of those prickly savages," he told Vanda, his pet bandrall.✱ "I'll send them after Officer Dork and his men. The soldiers will run for their lives when they see a hoard of Gorsemen charging at them! Come, Vanda, we're off to the moor. I shall go in disguise. From now on I can't be too careful. . ."

Dork hurried from the Kluster and selected a hundred soldiers to help him seize the wicked magician.

"We must be prepared for trouble," he told them. "You never know what to expect with Zorgan. We'll take the cannon. It hasn't been used for years, so it might be a bit rusty. Make sure it's in good working order and take plenty of mortar-melons."✱ ✱

✱ ✱
✱ **Bandrall** – rare flying mammal, native to Karisma
✱ ✱ **Mortar-melons** – ripe, round watermelons, traditional ammunition fired from Karisman cannon (mortar)

19

A soldier clicked his heels and saluted.

"Orders understood, sir!" he said.

For the next few hours, the palace was a scene of feverish activity, with everyone focused on the important task ahead. The soldiers cleaned the buttons on their uniforms and polished their boots till they could see their reflections in the toecaps. A gleaming cannon was mounted on a horse-drawn carriage, and several carts were loaded with melons.

By dawn the following day, the troops were assembled and ready to march.

Before they left, Queen Charm gave a rallying speech to speed them on their way:

"I have no doubt that dangers and difficulties lie ahead, but I am confident you'll succeed in your mission. Beware! The magician will be up to all kinds of tricks to avoid capture, but too much is at stake to allow Zorgan to remain free. The future happiness of Karisma rests with Sesame Brown and her quest to return my charm bracelet. Zorgan will do anything to get hold of it. Were that to happen, the consequences would be unthinkable! So, let no one stand in your way to bring the magician down. He must be caught at all costs! Setfair,* good soldiers. Have courage. May the luck of my charms, wherever they may be, go with you!"

* *
* Setfair – goodbye and good luck

21

Four

Sesame, Maddy, Gemma and Liz floated through the air, light as thistledown. For a while, they drifted over a bleak heart-shaped moor where nothing much grew except clumps of gorse; the bright, butter-yellow gorse flowers added colour to the landscape like splashes of paint on a picture.

Soon the girls were gently spiralling down to a rocky hill, where they landed near a cottage on the top. It seemed only seconds ago that they had been standing in Sesame's garden, and now they were worlds away in Karisma! The girls stood up and looked around.

Liz pushed her glasses firmly on her nose; everyone felt a little shaky. They appeared to be alone, apart from some speckled birds with long beaks and spiky crests near the cottage.

"I wonder where we are?" said Gemma.

"Heartmoor," said a voice right behind them.

The girls spun round, surprised to see a tiny, grey-haired woman who had appeared from nowhere. She had beady eyes, a beak-like nose and wore a ragged dress; perched on her head was a hat of feathers and over one arm she carried a basket. She shook Sesame warmly by the hand.

"Fairday,✶ Seeker Sesame," she said. "I'm Hesta the hermit, Gatekeeper Twelve. I've been expecting you."

How strange, thought Sesame. How did she know I was coming? I suppose anything's possible in Karisma! She greeted Hesta politely and introduced the others:

"These are my friends, Maddy Webb, Gemma Green and Liz Robinson."

"Hi," said Maddy.

* *
✶ Fairday – a typical Karisman friendly greeting

23

"Great to be back," said Gemma. "It's ages since we were here together." ✱

"Yeah," said Liz. "We're all Charmseekers."

"*Four* Charmseekers," said Hesta, as if the number was significant. "A good sign. Sit down. I have much to tell you."

While the gatekeeper seated herself on a bench, the girls sat around on the grass, eager to hear what she had to say. It was the summer mede of Mima, and the afternoon sun felt warm on their backs.

* *
✱ Do you remember when? You can follow the Charmseekers' exciting adventure in Book Eight: *Secret Treasure*

Hesta fed crumbs from her basket to the crested birds they'd seen earlier, then looked at Sesame with mock severity.

"Things have taken a turn for the worse, since your last visit," she began. "I'm afraid it's all your doing, Sesame Brown!"

"Oh!" cried Sesame. "What have I done?"

Hesta smiled.

"It's what you *haven't* done that matters," she said. "Zorgan is furious because you refused to bring him the charms. Brave girl! But he's taking it out on us. Him and his wretched spells!"

"What spells?" asked Maddy.

"Let me see," said Hesta. "A palace full of mice; a freak blizzard. Oh, and everyone's complaining about nightmares—"

"Ah," said Sesame, and she quickly told everyone about the one she'd had. "I guess Zorgan was responsible for that too."

"You *must* find the remaining charms," said Hesta. "The sooner Queen Charm has her bracelet back, the better. Only then will order be restored."

"We're looking for two more charms," said Sesame. "The cloverleaf and the key."

"I wonder which one we'll find first?" said Maddy.

Hesta had an inkling and replied in a riddle:

"Threes you'll see, the common kind;
The rarer fours are hard to find.
In flowery fields, 'tis my belief –
You'll spot the lucky . . .

". . . cloverleaf!" chorused the girls, jumping to their feet. She had given them a brilliant clue and they couldn't wait to start.

"Come on," said Sesame. "Let's go."

"Take care!" warned Hesta. "We are living in dangerous times. Her Majesty has ordered Officer Dork to capture Zorgan. The soldiers set out from the palace this morning. Zorgan will resist. He'll use curses, jinxes and all sorts to protect himself. It'll be quite a battle."

"Ooo!" said Maddy. "I hope we don't get zapped by a jinx."

Hesta rose to her feet and wished them well. She was halfway to her cottage, when Gemma remembered the gate and chased after her.

"What time do we have to be back?" she asked.

The gatekeeper pointed to the birds.

"Look for my friends," she said. "Return before you see twelve on my roof."

26

Five

Fearfully the Gorsemen watched the approach of an ominous dark cloud. They huddled in groups, each standing about four logs* high – about the height of a medium-sized troll; with their plump green bodies covered in prickles, they resembled a gathering of gooseberries.

* *

Log – the length of a log is used as a measurement in Karisma – equal to about 50cms in our world

The cloud
suddenly
twisted
itself
into a
tornado –
a violent
whirling
monster,
travelling
towards them
at alarming
speed. The force
of the wind
nearly blew them
off their feet. Two
Gorsemen, in particular,
were scowling at the sky –
their names were Craggs and
Spiker. As the tornado drew near, they
saw a face emerge from the gloomy mass.

"It's Zorgan!" said Craggs.

"What does *he* want?"
growled Spiker. "Haven't seen
the vermy* magician since he
put a curse on us."

* * * * * * * * * * * * * * * *
* **Vermy** – miserable worm

28

"Why *was* that exactly?" said Craggs. "It's so long ago, I've forgotten."

"Zorgan once pricked his finger on a gorse bush," said Spiker, keeping his voice low. "There happened to be some Gorsemen about, so he cursed us all with prickles. Horrible itchy things they are too!"

By now, Zorgan the tornado was hovering overhead, his voice thundered down to the Gorsemen below:

"There's work to do, my prickly friends! Do it well and you shall be rewarded."

"Hm! I wonder what sort of work *that* would be?" murmured Craggs.

"I think we're about to find out," said Spiker. "Here he comes."

Craggs and Spiker watched Zorgan spiral to the ground and shapeshift into himself. "A slight misunderstanding with the queen," said Zorgan.

"Charm has ordered Officer Dork and his men to . . . apprehend me. A ridiculous plan! But I'm sure I can rely on you to see them off."

This met with a good deal of disgruntled murmuring among the Gorsemen, until Spiker ventured to say:

"You mentioned a *reward*—"

"Quite so," said Zorgan. "Defeat Charm's soldiers and I'll lift my curse. A bargain, you'll agree?"

The Gorsemen weren't happy with the idea, but the thought of being relieved from their irritable skin condition *was* tempting. And so the deal was struck.

"Good, good," said Zorgan. "Prepare for battle straightaway. Oh, just one more thing. Keep your eyes open for a girl. She's an Outworlder.✶ I'm offering a handsome reward to anyone who brings me Sesame Brown!"

The following day, as a stream of Gorsemen left Heartmoor, on their way to ambush Dork's troops, Sesame and her friends were setting out to charm seek.

✶ ✶
✶ **Outworld** – the name Karismans call our world

"Where shall we start?" said Maddy.

"Look for some flowery fields," said Sesame, remembering the gatekeeper's riddle. "In flowery fields, 'tis my belief—"

"You'll spot the lucky cloverleaf!" sang out Liz and Gemma.

As they walked along, Sesame told her friends what had happened the last time she was in Karisma. It was a good opportunity to catch up on Charmseeker news. When Sesame got to the part where she went to Zorgan's Tower and came face to face with the magician, they all gasped.

"Oh, Ses!" cried Maddy. "You were SO lucky to escape."

"I know," said Sesame. "I was scared. Morbrecia was there too. She was really nice to me, so I suspected something weird was going on. In a funny way I feel sorry for her. After all she *is* the eldest sister. She's mad because Charm is queen. And I'm still not sure about the Silversmith . . ."

"I remember, you had a nightmare about *her*," said Gemma.

"We know loads of stuff about the Silversmith making the charms," said Liz. "If only we could see her."

"That's the problem," said Sesame, "I think I *did*. She was the beautiful woman in my nightmare with long, silvery hair and sparkling eyes.

31

But when I gave her the charm bracelet, she turned into a horrid witch!"

They had reached the edge of the moor and stopped to look around. Drifting overhead were some puffy white clouds. Sesame told the others about the one she'd seen from her window that morning, shaped like a cloverleaf.

"I knew it was a lucky sign," she said. "I'm sure we'll find the charm soon."

There was a faint smell of coconut from the gorse flowers in the air and, not far off, they saw fields of purple clover.

"Flowery fields!" chorused everyone happily, jumping up and down with delight.

"Great," said Sesame. "I'll race you there!"

Meanwhile, a band of Gorsemen (which included Craggs and Spiker) had been trundling over the clover fields; some were pushing handcarts full of gorse balls,* while others were struggling with a strange-looking piece of equipment on wheels. It was a catapult, designed to hurl flaming gorse balls over a considerable distance; it looked like a giant wooden spoon attached to ropes and pulleys, and it was called 'The Fiery Flinger'.

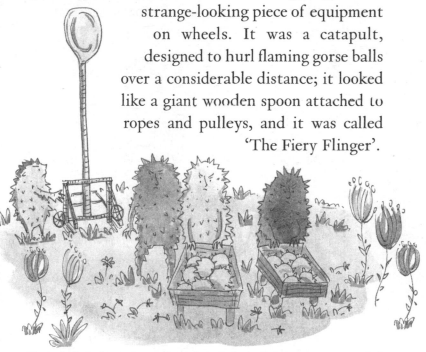

* **Gorse balls** — buds of the native Karisman gorse, which grow into large, spiky balls

However, the difficulty of manoeuvring the heavy contraption over ruts and hummocks, coupled with the itchiness of their skin, made the Gorsemen tired and crotchety, so they sat down to have a rest. Which is when they spotted four girls running their way . . .

"Vixee!" * exclaimed Spiker. "Outworlders!"

"Zorgan only mentioned one," said Craggs. "What was her name? Sumsunny Down . . ."

"Sesame Brown!" said Spiker. "But which one *is* Sesame? We don't know what she looks like."

"Ah," said Craggs. "I hadn't thought of that."

"Well, if we want to claim Zorgan's reward," said Spiker, "here's what we'll do . . ."

Clover grows tall as corn in Karisma, and soon the girls were waist-high in a sea of purple flowers.

"It'll take *ages* to find the charm in this lot," said Gemma, parting a way through the stems.

"I think someone's been here before us," said Maddy. "Look – wheel tracks."

* *
* **Vixee** – a gleeful, triumphant exclamation meaning 'great' or 'wicked'

34

The others saw where she was pointing.

"Some sort of cart by the looks of it," said Sesame, examining the freshly flattened plants.

"I wonder who— " began Liz and stopped.

They all heard a rustling noise, close by.

"Who's there?" they shouted.

There followed the sound of dry stalks snapping, and suddenly Sesame, Maddy, Gemma and Liz found themselves surrounded by Gorsemen. The bristly, green men looked most unfriendly, so the girls clung to each other for support.

"Which one of you is Sesame Brown?" Spiker demanded, his tone threatening.

Sesame was about to step forward, when Maddy held her back.

"I am!" declared Maddy boldly.

Immediately, Liz and Gemma cottoned on.

"No, I am," said Liz.

"It's me," said Gemma.

Sesame knew her friends were trying to help, but she couldn't let them take her place.

"*I'm* Sesame Brown!" she said firmly.

Spiker looked confused, until Craggs came up with a suggestion:

"I think it's the first one," he muttered.

"Right," whispered Spiker. "When I give the signal, grab her!"

While the Gorsemen were talking, the girls were plotting their next move.

"Let's make a run for it," said Sesame, keeping her voice low. "We'll split up to confuse them."

"Good idea," agreed Maddy.

"Okay," said Gemma and Liz.

"Ready," said Sesame.

"One, two, three . . . GO!"

At the very same moment, Spiker signalled to the waiting Gorsemen.

"After her!" he yelled.

And they tore after Maddy like a pack of hounds.

Hidden in the Clover

Can you find these nine words
hidden in the clover field?
Look for the words down, across,
diagonally and backwards.

SESAME

MADDY

GEMMA

LIZ

CLOVERLEAF

CHARM

SPIKER

CRAGGS

GORSEMEN

S	C	C	H	A	M	M	Y	P	E
E	L	S	G	G	A	R	C	M	I
M	O	A	A	C	D	D	A	Y	Z
A	V	M	L	C	H	S	O	V	M
S	E	I	I	Z	E	A	G	G	A
O	R	K	Z	S	M	K	R	Y	D
F	L	E	A	M	M	E	G	M	D
R	E	P	G	V	Z	I	R	A	Y
A	A	G	O	R	S	E	M	E	N
M	F	S	E	S	P	I	K	E	R

Six

In his Star Room, Zorgan peered through his powerful telescope, keeping a watchful eye on everything. He had witnessed the arrival of Sesame and the Charmseekers. He knew Craggs and Spiker would be tempted by a reward, and was sure it was only a matter of time before they delivered Sesame to his door.

In the meantime, he was pleased to see a large number of Gorsemen heading towards the tower, ready to defend him. Zorgan chuckled, thinking how easily he'd tricked them into believing he could lift the curse.

"The Prickly Curse is irreversible," he told his pixies, Nix and Dina, who were standing nearby. "By the time the Gorsemen learn the truth, it will be too late. If they cause trouble, I'll zap them with a spell. *Poof!* Bye bye, Gorsemen. Prickles and all!"

The pixics knew how ruthless the magician could be and stood there quaking in their shoes.

"You are very powerful, Master," said Nix.

"No one would dare challenge *you*," said Dina.

"Hm! Well, Queen Charm has done that very thing," said Zorgan. He swung the telescope in the direction of the palace. He could see a brigade of soldiers, their helmets glinting in the sunlight, marching his way. He was surprised at how many there were. A cruel smile curled his lips.

"Nix. Dina. Bring my spell books," he said. "Just Jinxes by Professor Brimstone and A Cauldron of Curses by Wizard Wanditch. Then let the fun begin!"

Shortly afterwards, there was a knock at the tower door. Zorgan opened a window and looked down to see Craggs and Spiker. They were standing by a handcart, looking very pleased with themselves.

"We've got Sesame Brown!" they shouted up to him.

"Spallah!" * cried Zorgan. "I knew I could rely on you."

So he ran down one hundred and ninety-five twisty steps and opened the door . . .

Maddy had spent an extremely unpleasant and uncomfortable journey in the handcart. Gagged, bound and lying under a heap of gorse balls, she had been jabbed so many times she felt like a pincushion. Suddenly the cart upended and she was dumped like a sack of coal on the doorstep. Craggs and Spiker proudly presented her to Zorgan, but they were shocked by the magician's reaction. He looked furious.

"Magworts!" ** Zorgan fumed. "You've got the wrong one!"

* *
* Spallah – excellent! a triumphant expression
** Magwort – probably the worst name you could call anyone! General term for a fool

Maddy, now lying helpless on the ground, watched as sparks flew from Zorgan's wand; the jinxes singed the Gorsemens' prickles. Craggs and Spiker hopped around yelping.

"Ouch!"   "Stop it."

"Oooo!"   "That hurt!"

Then everything happened at once. Maddy suddenly found herself bundled into the tower, along with Craggs and Spiker. She was vaguely aware of Nix and Dina; Zorgan was shouting and the pixies were obeying orders. They freed her from the ropes, then locked her in a room with the Gorsemen. When they had gone, Maddy tore off her gag and confronted her prickly companions.

"This is all your fault!" she said crossly.

"But you *said* you were Sesame," complained Craggs.

"Yeah, how were we supposed to know you weren't?" said Spiker indignantly. He rubbed his head where Zorgan had scorched him with a jinx. "You shouldn't tell lies."

"And maybe you shouldn't go around kidnapping people!" said Maddy.

For the next few minutes they glared at each other in silence. Maddy was angry and scared too, but she wasn't going to show the Gorsemen how she felt. She wondered where Sesame, Gemma and Liz were now. Would she *ever* see them again!

Craggs interrupted her thoughts.

"Zorgan promised us a reward for Sesame," he said miserably.

"*And* to lift his curse if we defended him," added Spiker, and told Maddy how all Gorsemen had come to be cursed. She couldn't help feeling sorry for them.

"How can you trust Zorgan after what he's done?" she said. "I bet he won't keep his side of the bargain. He's just using you."

Craggs and Spiker nodded.

"You may be right," they agreed.

The three then looked around for a way of escape.

They appeared to be in a dungeon, at the foot of the tower. Spiker tried the handle of the heavy wooden door, but it wouldn't budge. The walls were made of stone, but in one there was a crack; a shaft of sunlight streamed through from the outside, and that gave Maddy an idea. She fished in her pocket and produced a handkerchief with her initials embroidered in one corner.

"Pass me the rope," she said to Craggs. "I'll tie one end to my hanky. Push it through the crack. Someone may see it and rescue us." She hoped it would be Sesame.

For the time being, there was little more they could do, so they sat and talked. The Gorsemen were curious about Maddy and her friends – they'd never met any Outworlders before.

"Why did you come to Karisma?" asked Craggs.

"Tell us about Sesame Brown," said Spiker.

"Okay," said Maddy. "Oh, I'm Maddy by the way. There's Sesame, she's my best friend, and Gemma and Liz. We're in a secret club called the Charmseekers . . ."

Seven

Meanwhile, back in the clover field, Sesame, Gemma and Liz were becoming worried about Maddy. They'd eventually met up, having escaped capture by the prickly Gorsemen.

"You know Maddy, she's always late!" joked Gemma, trying to cheer everyone up.

"Maybe she's found the charm?" suggested Liz, not very convincingly.

Sesame tried to smile but, deep down, she knew something terrible had happened to her friend.

"I've seen loads of green men making for Zorgan's Tower," she said. "I have a nasty feeling the two we met have taken Maddy there."

"Oh, no," gasped Liz. "Poor Maddy!"

"Let's go after her," said Gemma.

"*I'm* going," said Sesame decisively. "They've taken Maddy hostage because they think she's me. If anyone's going to take risks, it had better be me."

"What shall *we* do?" said Liz, wiping clover pollen from her glasses.

"Look for the cloverleaf charm," said Sesame. "Please. You must find it."

"Cool," said Gemma. "We'll meet here later. Take care, Ses."

They gave each other their Charmseekers' hand sign for luck, then Sesame dashed away.

For a while, Sesame followed in the wake of the Gorsemen, keeping well out of sight. Soon she skirted the Dark Forest, which lay to her left then, spotting a clear line of cart tracks, she made straight for the tower.

It wasn't long before she caught up with the last of Queen Charm's soldiers, marching briskly along a road. Bringing up the rear was someone she recognised at once. It was Officer Dork.

"Oh, no," groaned Sesame. "Just my luck."

Her first instinct was to hide. Dork had accused her of stealing the charms several times before and had even attempted to arrest her once. She was relieved when he greeted her cheerfully.

"Fairday, Sesame Brown!" he said, slowing his pace, so she could march beside him.

"Hi," said Sesame.

In the distance they heard explosions and saw bursts of orange light streaking across the sky.

"The battle's begun," said Dork. "We were expecting trouble from the magician. But we shall bravely face whatever dangers lie ahead. No place for a girl like you, eh?"

Sesame rolled her eyes and ignored his last remark.

"I think my friend Maddy has been abducted and taken to Zorgan's Tower," she said. "I'm on my way to rescue her."

Dork looked horrified.

"Who'd do a thing like that?"

"Some prickly green men—" she began.

Dork stopped dead in his tracks.

"P-p-p-prickly green men," he said. "D-d-do you m-m-mean G-G-G-GORSEMEN?"

"I don't know," said Sesame. "Anyway, whoever they were they really wanted me. But Maddy said *she* was me so they took her away by mistake."

Dork looked confused, but he was under strict orders to protect Sesame.

"Allow me to escort you to the tower," he said, with a click of his heels. "Officer Dork at your service!"

While they marched along, Sesame told Dork about the Charmseekers.

"We've only two more charms to find," she said. "Then I can return Queen Charm's bracelet."

"Her Majesty is looking forward to meeting you," said Dork. "She is relying on you to save Karisma!"

"I can't wait to meet *her*," said Sesame happily. "I saw Queen Charm on Agapogo Day.* I was running away from her sister! She's after the charms too, you know."

"Ah, Princess Morbrecia!" said Dork with a faraway look in his eyes. He had always been in awe of the queen's rebellious sister, and just a little afraid. "I think Her Highness is under Zorgan's spell. The sooner we deal with HIM the better!"

* *
* **Agapogo Day** – a holiday in honour of Agapogo, the dragon of the Silver Pool. Do you remember what happened? You can read Sesame's adventure in Book Three: *The Dragon's Revenge*

From her castle that same morning, Morbrecia saw the soldiers marching northwards to the tower. She was going there herself and had ordered her footmen to make ready her carriage.

Earlier, Morbrecia had received a strange message from her enchanted doll, Elmo. Zorgan had given Morbrecia the doll when she was six years old and ever since, Morbrecia had refused to part with her. Zorgan had often used the doll as a way to communicate with Morbrecia, but today was different. Today, it wasn't Zorgan's voice she heard, or Zorgan's words tumbling from Elmo's lips. The voice was high, chillingly cold and clear, and the words were unmistakably Elmo's own!

"Zorgan, this day, shall be no more,
So hasten to the wizard's door.
Fly to where the wizard dwells,
His crystal ball and books of spells
Are there and for the taking.
Soon you'll be magic making!"

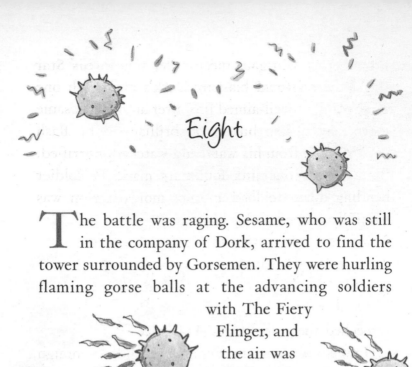

Eight

The battle was raging. Sesame, who was still in the company of Dork, arrived to find the tower surrounded by Gorsemen. They were hurling flaming gorse balls at the advancing soldiers with The Fiery Flinger, and the air was thick with smoke and heat.

Despite the danger, Sesame couldn't help smiling to herself as she thought of her dad's barbeque, and suddenly home seemed very far away.

The soldiers retaliated with mortar-melons, which they fired from a cannon; the melons smashed against the tower on impact and showered the Gorsemen with slushy goo.

52

Zorgan, meanwhile, was in his Star Room blasting Dork's men with one well-aimed jinx after another. Sesame saw bursts of brilliant light flash from his wand and watched, horrified, as one jinx found its mark. A soldier bending down to load another mortar-melon was painfully zapped on his bottom.

"Yeeeeeowooooo!"

screeched the unfortunate man.

However, when some soldiers were brave enough to recklessly charge at a band of Gorsemen, Sesame saw her chance to get to the tower. She charged with them, ducking and diving to avoid a hail of

stinging jinxes, until she reached the door.

That was when she caught sight of Maddy's handkerchief, fluttering from a crack in the wall.

Sesame knew it must belong to Maddy; her initials, MW, were embroidered in a corner.

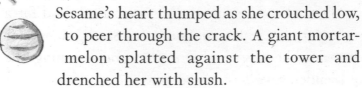

Sesame's heart thumped as she crouched low, to peer through the crack. A giant mortar-melon splatted against the tower and drenched her with slush.

"Maddy!" she shouted, above the noise of the battlefield.

"Ses!" came Maddy's immediate reply. "I can't believe you're here!"

"I'll get you out," promised Sesame. "But I have to see Zorgan first."

"Oh, Ses," said Maddy. "*Please* be careful!"

Down in the dungeon, although she knew Sesame couldn't see her, Maddy made their secret hand-sign and wished her good luck.

Dork's men rammed the tower door and smashed it to the ground. They had been wrestling with some Gorsemen and their hands were full of prickles. Sesame dashed past them and through the doorway. She sprinted up the twisty stairs and halfway up, she met Nix and Dina flying down.

54

"My master wants to see you," said Nix.

"Come with us," said Dina.

"Out of my way," Sesame yelled, pushing them aside. "I don't need your help."

She tore to the top of the tower and stood for a moment, breathless outside the Star Room. Her legs felt like jelly and her tummy was churning like a blender. She was scared — more frightened than she had ever been in her life — but she knew she had to confront Zorgan. She fingered her locket, held it for a second or two and felt it warm and tingly to her touch. Inside were the pictures of her parents, and thinking of them gave her courage. Then she pushed open the door and went inside.

Zorgan had his back to her, firing powerful jinxes from the window at the soldiers below. He screamed with delight when he hit one. Sesame stood rooted to the spot at the sight that met her eyes.

The Star Room was a fascinating place, full of weird and wonderful things for making magic; spell books, potions, a clockwork universe, flickering candles, a crystal ball . . .

Zorgan suddenly wheeled round and saw her standing there. His black eyes glinted.

"At last," he said. "I knew you'd come looking for your friend. Such loyalty is admirable in one so young— "

"Release Maddy!" demanded Sesame. "It's me you want, not her."

"Quite so," said Zorgan, pausing to fire yet another jinx from the window. There was a jet of light, followed by a **Bang!** and the distant howl of someone in pain. "But first we must strike a bargain. You will be familiar with my terms. I see you are wearing your pretty locket. Good. The very thing."

Sesame shivered. The magician's tone was creepy – like hairy spiders crawling down her spine.

"I'll free your friend in return for your promise," said Zorgan. "Swear on your mother's name you will bring me the bracelet!"

"No way!" shouted Sesame, finding courage she didn't know she had.

Zorgan was furious, his patience with this stubborn girl expired. He aimed his wand at her and screamed:

"Promise or you'll be sorry"

"NO!" yelled Sesame. "NEVER!"

There was a blinding flash.
An ear-splitting

Crack!

"Ooooof!" went Sesame as the jinx hit her locket like a thunderbolt. The force of it threw her to the floor. She felt the floor shake, the tower tremble. And then she heard the terrible wail of Zorgan in agony.

"Aaaargh! No. NO! This cannot be happening. I must . . . have . . . the bracelet. A thousand curses on you, Sesame Brown! AAAARGH—"

Dazed, Sesame struggled to her feet. She heard a *hiss!* and thought it was a snake. Nervously she looked around on the floor, but there was nothing there.

Where Zorgan had been standing, a pall of black smoke now coiled slowly upwards and out through the window. Zorgan the magician was no more. Sesame stood there shaking. She blinked and blinked, unable to comprehend what had happened. What *had* happened? she wondered. She wasn't sure. All she knew was that Zorgan had gone and somehow she'd survived the powerful jinx. She couldn't believe her luck.

Sesame raced back down the spiral staircase, two at a time. At the bottom she found Nix and Dina, frozen like statues and staring out at her from unseeing, crystal eyes. The pixies, who'd been created by Zorgan, could not survive without their master. Their steely wings would fly no more. Phew! I'm glad they won't be bothering me again, thought Sesame, as she ran outside.

The roar of battle had been replaced by loud cheering from both sides. She was trying to make sense of it all, when Maddy ran up to her and flung her arms around her.

"Ses! You did it. You did it!" she cried.

"Did what?" said Sesame, hugging her friend and wondering how she'd escaped from the dungeon.

Then everyone was talking at once.

"Zorgan disappeared in a puff of smoke!"

"Look. My prickles have gone!"

"Hooray! So have mine."

There was much laughter and back-slapping among the soldiers and the Gorsemen. They had lost their prickles when the curse magically disappeared with Zorgan. No one noticed a carriage drawn up at the side of the tower, nor the woman in a hooded cloak slipping inside. No one that is, except a little bird, and she flew away to tell the Silversmith.

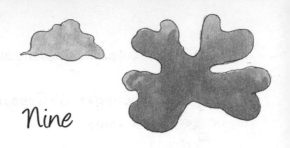

Nine

Meanwhile, far away in the clover field, Gemma and Liz had been searching for the cloverleaf charm. It was like looking for a needle in a haystack.

"I wonder if Sesame's found Maddy?" said Liz, peering under yet another clump of clover.

"If anyone can, Ses can," said Gemma "Sesame Brown will track her down."

She stopped for a moment to look at a cloud.

"You won't find the charm up there," said Liz.

"Look," said Gemma. "See what I see?"

Liz adjusted her glasses and stared at the cloud.

"Well, I suppose it looks a bit like—"

"A cloverleaf!" said Gemma. "Remember what Sesame said? She saw one like it this morning. It must be a clue."

"Wicked!" said Liz.

The two girls ran through the field of clover, until they were standing below the cloud.

"Start looking," said Gemma. "We haven't been here before."

It took about another twenty minutes of crawling around on their hands and knees, before Liz yelled: "Found it!"

The perfect little cloverleaf charm was caught up in a tangle of weeds, glistening in the sun. Carefully Liz reached in and picked it up.

"Wow," said Gemma. "It's lovely."

They stood, taking it in turns to hold the magical charm, admiring its delicate design.

"Ses will be pleased," said Liz, proud to have been the one to find it.

Just then they heard voices calling to them.

"Gemma! Liz! Where are you?"

"They're back!" chorused the girls, recognising Sesame and Maddy's voices.

Liz clutched the cloverleaf charm in her hand, then together they raced across the field to meet them. They were astonished at the sight that met their eyes. There were Sesame and Maddy, riding on a weird machine on wheels, surrounded by the green men, who had caused all the trouble in the first place – only now the men no longer had any prickles and they looked very friendly.

Sesame and Maddy jumped down and hugged their friends.

"We've got SO much to tell you," she said, her eyes shining.

"And we've got something to tell *you*," said Liz, opening her palm.

"Yesss!" cried Sesame punching the air. She held up the silver cloverleaf for Maddy to see.

Maddy beamed, then she caught sight of the gatekeeper's cottage, high on the hill.

"The birds! We must get back to the gate," she cried.

Spiker stepped forward.

"I've got an idea," he said.

Minutes later, the four girls were sitting on the The Fiery Flinger, waiting for take-off.

"Ready?" shouted Spiker.
They took a deep breath.
"Fire!" yelled Craggs.

"Weeeeeeeeeee!"

screamed the Charmseekers, all the way
back to the gate.

"Hurry!" cried Hesta. "The gate is
closing."

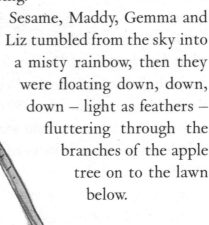

Sesame, Maddy, Gemma and
Liz tumbled from the sky into
a misty rainbow, then they
were floating down, down,
down – light as feathers –
fluttering through the
branches of the apple
tree on to the lawn
below.

Nic was by the barbeque, brandishing a sausage on the end of a long fork.

"Food's ready," he called out to the girls, as if they'd been chatting for ages. "You must be hungry after all that gossiping!"

✳ ✳ ✳

Later that evening, after everyone had gone home, Sesame got ready for bed. She sat for a while in her room, thinking about what had happened. It had been an extraordinary day; she'd woken from a frightening nightmare, then there was the drama at the stables and it had ended with an adventure in Karisma. Sesame wondered how much longer it would be before she could tell her father, her grandmother, and Jodie – everyone who meant so much to her – about her secret, magical world. One day soon she knew she'd *have* to tell them . . .

She felt in her pocket and fished out the precious cloverleaf charm. The beautiful four-leafed clover nestled in the palm of her hand, glistening with a silvery light of its own. She recalled the gatekeeper's words, when they'd first arrived: '*Four* Charmseekers' she had said, as if the number meant something special. It did. Four *was* a lucky number!

The four of them had helped each other; Maddy had tried to protect her; Gemma and Liz had found the charm and, although she didn't really understand how, *she* had defeated Zorgan and helped everyone! It seemed too good to be true. She glanced in her wardrobe mirror, half-expecting a terrifying vision of Zorgan to leap out at her, but there was nothing there except her own reflection.

Sesame opened her special jewellery box and took out the silver bracelet; then she fastened the cloverleaf charm securely to the band and held it up to the light.

"Twelve magical charms," she told her teddy, Alfie. "Only one more to find and my quest is over."

She had just closed the lid, when her mobile jingled. There was a message from a number she didn't recognise.

HI SESAME. THANK U FOR HELPING MISTY. JODIE SAYS U WERE BRILL! VERY SOZ U MISSED UR RIDE. CU. LUV OLIVIA X

THAT'S OK. GLAD 2 HELP. SESAME ☺

Sesame switched off her mobile. Yes, she thought. It's been an amazing day.

Ten

O fficer Dork has told me everything," said Charm. "I can't believe Zorgan has gone forever."

"Destroyed by his own jinx," said the Silversmith. She allowed herself a wry smile. "I felt the shock of it myself. The jinx rebounded off Sesame's locket, which made it exceptionally powerful. Not even Zorgan could survive it."

"Quisto!"* exclaimed Charm. "I'm so thankful Sesame escaped unharmed."

It was the day after the battle at Zorgan's Tower, and the two women were walking in the palace gardens. They had entered the maze and were walking along the narrow, grassy paths that went round in circles, until at last they reached the smallest circle in the middle. At the centre stood a large stone pot, planted with bright red poppies.

* *

Quisto – an exclamation of surprise

"This is where it all began," said the Silversmith
wistfully. "This is where Sesame found your
bracelet with the heart charm, remember?"

"Of course," said Charm. "It seems such a long
time ago. Do you think Sesame will return my
bracelet soon?"

"I believe so," said the Silversmith. "She has only
one more charm to find. The little silver key, but—"

"But what?" said Charm, detecting a hint of
caution in her tone.

"Sesame still has to *find* the key, Your Majesty,"
said the Silversmith. "And dangers still lie in her
path. A little bird told me that Morbrecia has taken
possession of Zorgan's most dangerous spell books!

She has his crystal ball too. Your sister has always had a fascination for Dark Magic. I fear she may become a powerful sorceress."

Charm was shocked. She couldn't begin to understand how the Silversmith had learned all this about her sister, but the thought of Morbrecia making magic and mayhem was alarming, to say the least.

"It all started when Zorgan gave her that wretched doll!" she said.

"Elmo?" said the Silversmith. "I remember you telling me about her. You thought she tried to kill you!"✶

"Yes," said Charm. "And *you* thought Elmo possessed supernatural powers. She's been a bad influence on Morbrecia, ever since. It would explain why she stole my bracelet. Why she's tried to stop Sesame finding my charms."

"I think Zorgan is to blame, not Morbrecia," said the Silversmith gently. "I don't believe your sister is really wicked or means you harm. She fell under Zorgan's spell when she was very young—"

"Zorgan *again*," said Charm, exasperated. "Will I never hear the last of that balam✶✶ magician?"

* *
✶ Do you remember what happened? You can read Charm's story in Book Four: *A Tale of Two Sisters*
✶✶ **Balam** – cursed, an angry exclamation

Later, when the Silversmith returns to her workshop on Mount Fortuna, she looks at the thirteen magic candles. The candle that bears the name of the cloverleaf has flickered and died. Now only one solitary candle glows, burning brightly for its missing charm.

"Where is the key? The key!" she whispers to the candle. She presses her fingertips to her temples, closes her eyes and focuses her mystic energies on her Seeker, far beyond the boundaries of Karisma. "Sesame must return and find the thirteenth charm. Then all will be well."

A million thoughts flit through her head like fireflies, and she knows what she must do. Few possess, as she does, the magic power to 'transworld'; she has transported herself to the Outworld once before and, when the time is right, she will go there again . . .

But that's another story! It must be told another day.

Acknowledgments

I owe a debt of gratitude to all those who have worked behind the scenes at Orion Children's Books and beyond to bring the *Charmseekers* books and their thirteen delightful charms to you. Since it would take more space than this edition allows to mention individuals by name, suffice it to say that I'm hugely grateful to my publishers and everyone involved with the publication of this series. In particular, my special thanks go to: my publisher, Fiona Kennedy, for her faith in believing I could write way beyond my own expectations. Her creative, tactful and skilful editing kept Sesame Brown on the right track and helped me to write a better story; my agent, Rosemary Sandberg; Jenny Glencross and Jane Hughes (Editorial); Alex Nicholas and Helen Speedy (Rights) Loulou Clark and Helen Ewing (Design); Clare Hennessy (Production); Jessica Killingley and Jo Dawson (Marketing); Pandora White (Orion Audio Books); Imogen Adams (Website designer – www.hammerinheels.com); Neil Pymer, the *real* Spinner Shindigs, for kind permission to use his name; and last, but by no means least, a million thanks go to my husband Tom for his inexhaustible patience, critical appraisal and support along the way.

Georgie Adams